The Tale of Despereaux™

THE GRAPHIC NOVEL

Adapted and illustrated by
MATT SMITH *and* DAVID TILTON

Based on the motion picture screenplay

Based on the book by KATE DiCAMILLO

CANDLEWICK PRESS

First edition 2008

Library of Congress Cataloging-in-Publication Data is available.

Library of Congress Catalog Card Number 2008932000

ISBN 978-0-7636-4312-6

2 4 6 8 10 9 7 5 3 1

Printed in the United States of America

This book was typeset in Formal 436.
The illustrations were digitally created.

Candlewick Press
99 Dover Street
Somerville, Massachusetts 02144

visit us at www.candlewick.com

In Dor, Christmas was nothing. Well, they still celebrated it, but it was nothing compared to...

On the first Sunday of every spring, Dorians young and old would flock toward the castle...

to hear the official royal soup announced.

8

Now, a big part of being a genius is making everyone *believe* that you are.

And sometimes that takes a little help.

There are all kinds of genies. Some are in lamps...

some are in bottles...

but, of course, where else would a soup genie be but in a cookbook?

FZZZT!

POOF!

9

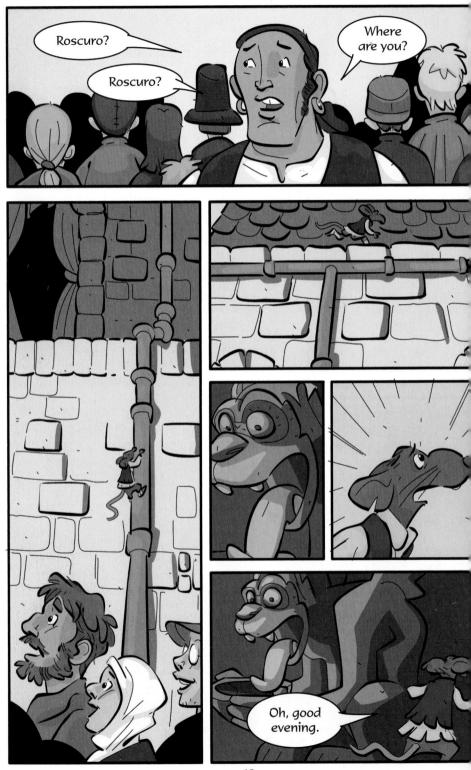

13

16

From this moment on, soup—the making of soup, the selling of soup, or the eating of soup—is hereby banned in the Kingdom of Dor.

Furthermore, rats are to be considered illegal as well and are hereby deemed unlawful creatures in the Kingdom of Dor.

From this moment on, anyone caught harboring, sheltering, or possessing a rat in any way shall face the full wrath of the law.

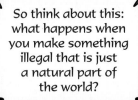

So think about this: what happens when you make something illegal that is just a natural part of the world?

You may as well make flies illegal... or sweat...or Monday morning.

But that's just what the king did—

out of a terrible sadness.

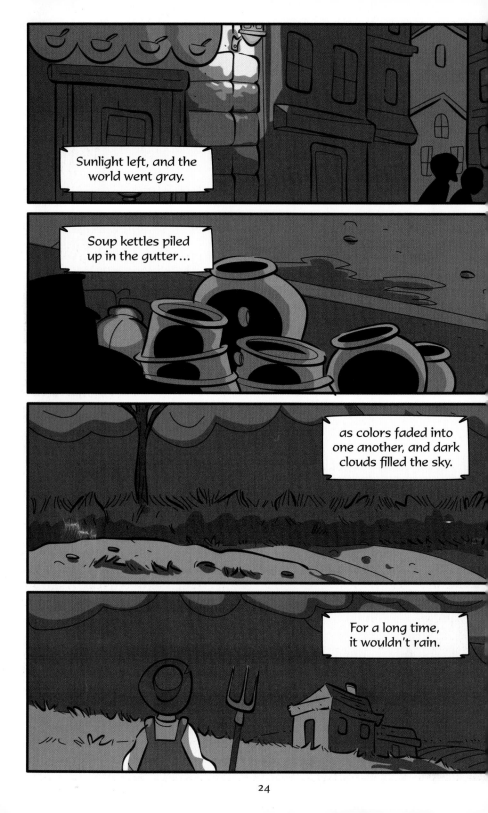

Princess Pea watched the never-changing landscape from the window of her room.

I wish it would rain, Louise.

You an' the whole world, madam.

Now, stay still. Almost finished fixi your lovely dress.

Louise, do you think there's a bit of light somewhere in the world?

Dunno, ma'am.

I think there is. You just need to know where to find it.

27

and Mrs. Tilling met with
Despereaux's teacher to
discuss his behavior....

We're worried about him.

He doesn't scurry.
He doesn't cower. At first we
thought he would grow out
of it, but...

Some kids are slower than
others. He'll cower in time.
We'll work on it.

Yes, but—

It'll be fine.
I promise.

You can send in
your son now.

32

He-llo-o...

He-llo-o...

Despereaux's call echoed in the darkness of the void below.

Far off in the gloom, a horrible singing filled the air...

Stinky, dark and foul and rotting, oozing sores and blood that's clotting. Mmm! Delicious! Hits the spot! It's great to be a rat!

When we see a chained-up victim, our hearts bleed—and then we lick him. Chew his ears and nose—THEY picked him. We're just being rats!

35

Roscuro hurried away from the other rats. Botticelli was right; Roscuro was missing something.

He glanced in either direction as he reached his secret hiding place, a chink in the masonry of the stone wall.

a narrow shaft of light.

It was nothing but a small crevice in the castle's construction, but from there Roscuro could see...

It was very faint, but Roscuro basked in the dim glow of the small beam.

39

The Royal Library

You start by nibbling along the edge of the page....The glue is all right, but it's the pages that taste best.

You're not supposed to *read* it! You're supposed to *eat* it!

Once upon a time...

Ooooh, that sounds great!

OK, I'll come back in an hour.

And no reading! It's a rule!

As soon as Furlough was gone, Despereaux turned his attention back to the story....

The spell of the story was suddenly broken by the sound of music from somewhere nearby....

Despereaux followed the music down a long hallway.

He listened as the same sad refrain was played over and over.

Princess Pea was also listening to her father playing his mournful song.

Then she turned away, saddened, for the king was lost in grief and would not leave his room.

Pea returned to her chamber, not knowing that she was being followed by a tiny mouse.

45

46

HA-HAAA!

As Despereaux flew down the hallway in pure bliss, he didn't notice the servant scrubbing the floor on her hands and knees.

Now, there are all kinds of princesses: some are born that way, some marry into it, and me are destined to be princesses only in their own minds...

but at one time or another, almost every little girl longs to be a princess.

51

Back at the library, Despereaux delved back into the story...for himself— and for the princess!

But what he didn't know was that he had been followed...

DESPEREAUX TILLING!

by the Mouse Council!

How long have you been working on this book?

Um... a week?

A week? You've hardly started it.

Well...I was... I just wanted to see how it ends.

Despereaux was brought before the Mouse Council to hear the charges against him.

...Refused training as a mouse, refused to respect the will and guidance of elder mice, repeatedly engaged in bold and unmeek behavior...

had personal contact with...

a human being!

Despereaux Tilling, are these charges true?

Yes. I think so.

Do you understand the penalty for associating or conversing with a human being?

who will prepare you for your descent into the unknown world. You shall be exiled—alone—into the dungeons of Dor...

from which no use and no light has ever escaped.

Hovis the Threadmaster emerged from the shadows....

So you're the "brave" one.

I guess.

That's good. It'll carry well down there.

Hovis unraveled a length of thread from the spool he carried.

Wear this proudly. There's no shame.

Despereaux untied the thread and left it behind as he turned toward the darkness. He jumped back quickly, startled by the shape looming beside him— the skull of an unlucky prisoner.

Hello? Hello?

Gregory the jailer answered.

Who is that?

Who goes there?

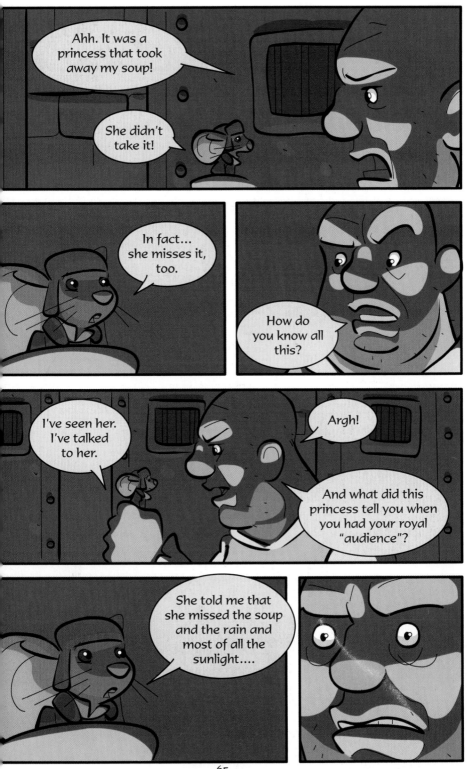

65

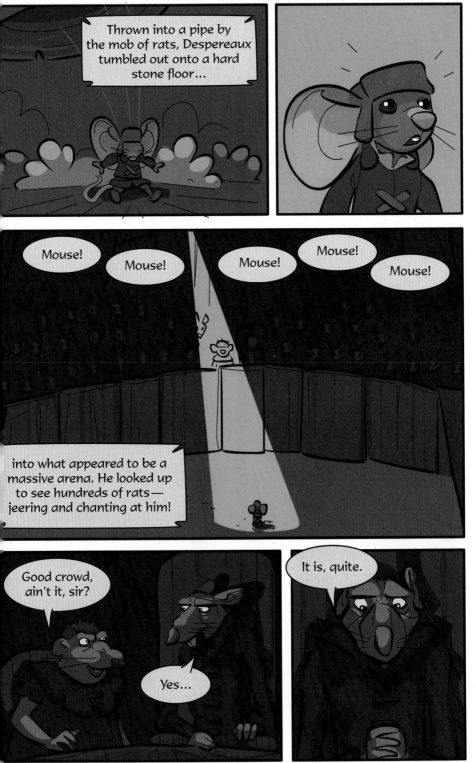

68

71

72

Over the next few weeks, Despereaux told Roscuro everything he knew about loyalty and honor and chivalry and courage. He told him about the princess and where her longing came from—that she missed the rain and the soup and even the rats....

He told him about the code of honor. About his noble quest. About duty and loyalty. And there in the darkness of the dungeon...

Even the rats?

two "knights" pledged devotion to a princess who was trapped inside a castle...

trapped in a life full of pain and longing.

And so the next time Mig returned to the kitchen with the empty dishes, she also took along something extra...

something Mig could not see hidden under the napkin. Something small yet determined...

something—or someone—on a noble quest to set his wrongs to right!

In the cluttered broom closet, Roscuro wandered aimlessly toward an empty pail.

He caught his reflection in the curved and pitted surface. He looked mottled and grotesque.

How would YOU feel if your own name was a bad word?

Well, that's how Roscuro felt about who he was—a rat.

When your heart breaks, it can grow back crooked. It can grow back twisted, gnarled, and hard.

Roscuro still had "longing," but now he just longed for someone whose heart was hardened...

87

Hurt is a funny thing. The same thing that makes one person angry can make another person sad.

Many years earlier...

Ned, take care of my little princess....

I can't no more.

Oh, aye, Gregory. I will.

Don't worry.

I'm sorry So, so sorr

When the blanket slipped, a heart-shaped birthmark was revealed on the little girl. Gregory always said she had too much heart...

88

90

In another cell, a second prisoner cries out.

You filthy stinking rat!

Events did not turn out as Miggery Sow had hoped.

You tricked me!

No crown. No special dresses. Instead she found herself in a dark cell.

Meanwhile, Despereaux finds his way up to the window of Pea's cell.

Milady?

Psst... milady.

Oh, my little mouse!

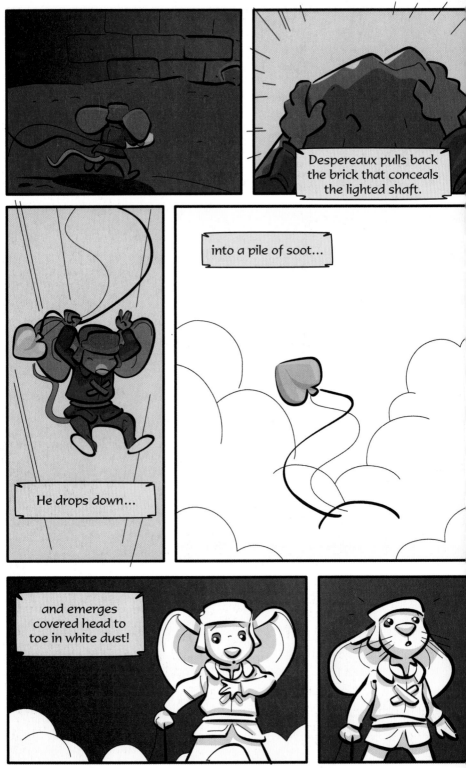

Despereaux pulls back the brick that conceals the lighted shaft.

He drops down...

into a pile of soot...

and emerges covered head to toe in white dust!

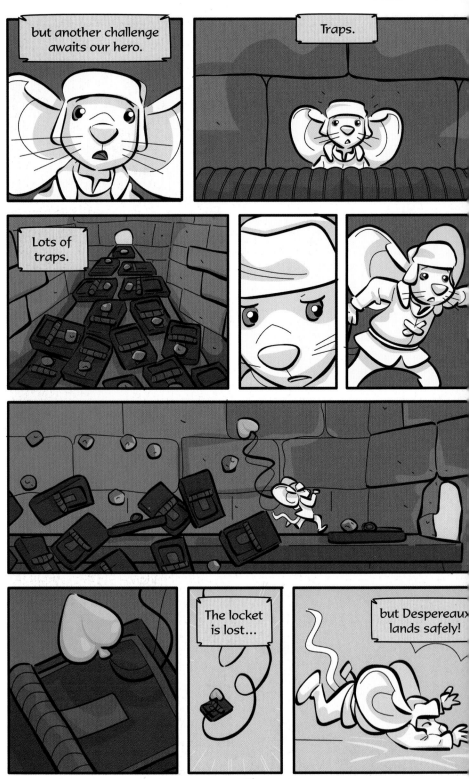

106

Meanwhile, Gregory makes his rounds rough the dungeon....

CLINK
CLINK

I'mmm in heeere!

Hearing a muffled call for help, he looks into the cell...

and recognizes a heart-shaped rthmark that could belong to only one person—

his princess.

Gor, what took you so long? I been screamin' in here for hours.

Arriving just as the rats swarm Pea, Despereaux searches for a way to save her.

The cat cage!

High above is the winch that opens the cage...

Gasp!

EEEEEAAAKKK!

MMMMFFF!

He lets the furious beast loose!

116

Pulling himself up, Despereaux finds he is not alone.

If it isn't our brave little knight. And it seems he came just in time for dinner.

Hmmm. I wonder, should I finish you off myself...

or turn you into cat food?

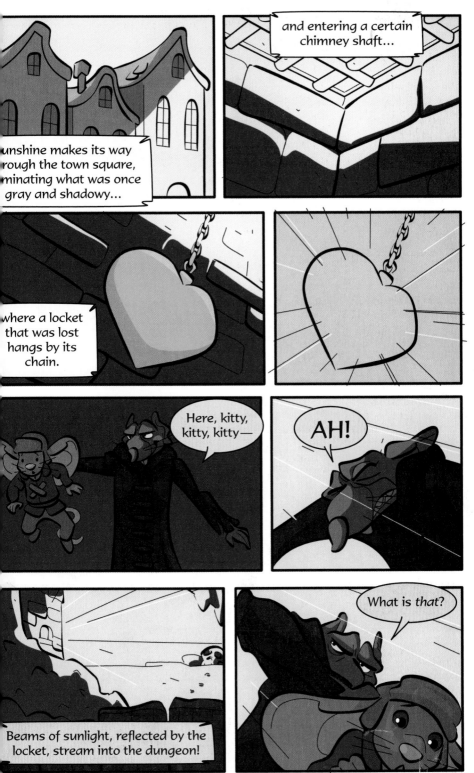

With the coliseum free of rats and full of light, Despereaux is able to untie Pea.

Thank you, my good gentleman.

Roscuro slowly approaches Despereaux and Pea.

I am sorry.

A smile breaks across Roscuro's face as a weight lifts from his heart.

You have nothing to be sorry about.

At the same time, Gregory embraces Mig in a giant bear-hug.

I'm so, so sorry. You have no idea how sorry I am.

Mig clutches her father, filled with a strange new emotion.

The citizens of Dor flood the city streets, exuberant in the sunlight.

The king, looking on as his subjects and his kingdom return to life, speaks quietly, almost to himself....

I'm so sorry.

Turning away from the window, the king smiles as he looks across the room at the queen's portrait.

So, you could call all of this a big misunderstanding if you wanted to. A king was hurt, so he hurt a rat. And a rat was hurt, so he hurt a princess....

And a princess was hurt...

so she hurt a servant girl without even meaning to do it....

And that servant had been hurting for so long that almost nothing could make her feel better.

And the people of Dor lived side by side with their rats....

All except one...

who went back to sea and felt cool breezes each morning and the sun on his face every afternoon.

We'd tell you that they all lived happily ever after...